Grizzly's Home

and Other Northwest Coast Children's Stories

Written and Illustrated
by
Robert James Challenger

Heritage House Publishing Company Ltd.
#108 – 17665 66A Avenue
Surrey, BC V3S 2A7
www.heritagehouse.ca

Library and Archives Canada Cataloguing in Publication
Challenger, Robert James, 1953–
    Grizzly's home and other Northwest Coast children's stories / Robert James Challenger.—1st ed.

    ISBN 978-1-894384-94-0

    1. Children's stories, Canadian (English) 2. Nature stories, Canadian (English) I. Title.

PS8555.H277G74 2005   jC813'.54   C2005-904129-3

All illustrations: Robert James Challenger
Book design and layout: Darlene Nickull
Editor: Ursula Vaira

Printed in Canada

 **Mixed Sources**
Cert no. SW-COC-001271
© 1996 FSC
FSC

This book has been printed with FSC-certified, acid-free papers, processed
chlorine free and printed with vegetable based inks.

Heritage House acknowledges the financial support for its publishing program from the
Government of Canada through the Book Publishing Industry Development Program (BPIDP),
Canada Council for the Arts, and the British Columbia Arts Council.

 Canada Council   Conseil des Arts
for the Arts   du Canada

 BRITISH COLUMBIA
ARTS COUNCIL
Supported by the Province of British Columbia

Dedication

This book is dedicated to my daughters, Kristi and Kari.

Whenever I think of people I admire,
I think of you.

Acknowledgements

The author acknowledges the following friends for their assistance and advice on the stories within this book.

Joannie Challenger, B.Ed.
Teacher, Hans Helgesen Elementary School
Metchosin, B.C.

Heather Owen, M.Ed.
District Counselling Psychologist
Sooke School District #62

Julie Wilmott, M.Ed.
Principal, Savory Elementary School
Langford, B.C.

Other books by Robert James Challenger

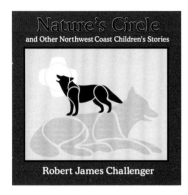

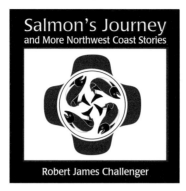

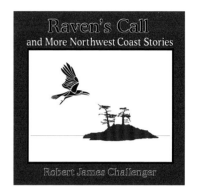

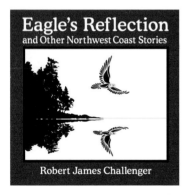

Nature's Circle
and Other Northwest Coast Children's Stories
ISBN 978-1-894384-77-3

Salmon's Journey
and More Northwest Coast Stories
ISBN 978-1-894384-34-6

Raven's Call
and More Northwest Coast Stories
ISBN 978-1-895811-91-9

Eagle's Reflection
and Other Northwest Coast Stories
ISBN 978-1-895811-07-0

Orca's Family
and More Northwest Coast Stories
ISBN 978-1-895811-39-1

All $9.95

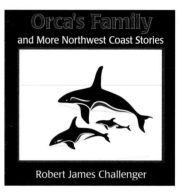

Wonderful Northwest Coast stories for kids ... Jim Challenger is a real artist as his book demonstrates.

—Ron MacIssac, Shaw Cable's "What's Happening?"

I really loved your stories that you read to us. I really got the feeling of what you meant in your magical writing. Thank you for coming to our school to make us feel joyful. I enjoyed your stories!! Sincerely,

—Josey L. (Age 8)

Modern day fables are the right length ... knows how to write for the oral storyteller; the written words slip easily off the tongue.

—*Times Colonist*

Challenger's prose bears a deliberate resemblance to First Nations oral traditions: humans and nature interact freely, and both are capable of folly, repentance, and wisdom. In his artwork, Challenger also embraces West Coast Aboriginal culture by portraying his characters in exquisite Haida-style prints. Highly recommended.

—Steve Pitt, *Canadian Book Review Annual*

Contents

Grizzly's Home

Two little girls sat with their mother in front of the fire. Around them were other members of their family, all with the warm light of the flames reflecting on their faces. Mother looked down at her daughters and lovingly brushed a wisp of hair from one of their faces.

They talked about their day. One of the girls said, "I really enjoyed going for a walk along the beach with everyone, even though winter's wind has been cold."

The other girl said, "It's nice having such a wonderful warm home to come back to after our walk."

Mother said, "I'm glad you feel safe and secure. One of the most important things we give to others is the feeling of being safe in the place we live.

"Many years ago Grandfather told me the story of Grizzly Bear and how he taught her that feeling safe is one of the best gifts you can give to someone."

"Tell us the story!" said the two girls.

"Well," said Mother, "Grizzly Bear lived in a valley not far from here. She roamed about, and because she was so big, she never had to be afraid of any other animals. That is, until a group of mean people came to live in the same valley.

"These people did not care about anyone but themselves. They did not care if they took all the fish the bears needed to eat. They did not care if they cut down the trees the bears needed for shelter. And they did not care if they killed a bear just to get its fur or claws.

"One day Grizzly Bear ran into some of them out hunting, and they started to shoot at her. She ran and hid in her den. For the first time in her life she was scared, both for herself and for the unborn cubs that were growing inside her.

"Now she could no longer enjoy the place she called home. When she was out looking for food, she was always hoping the mean people wouldn't hurt her. Even when she was in her den she worried they would find her.

"She didn't want to be in a place where she didn't feel safe, so she decided to leave, and she went over the mountain ridge and came to this valley, where Grandfather lived.

7

"When they first met, Grizzly Bear was afraid that Grandfather would try to hurt her, like the others had. But Grandfather knew the importance of making others around you feel safe.

"Grandfather shared his fish with Grizzly Bear, so she could build up her strength again. He showed her the best places to find berries, so she could store up energy for her hibernation.

"Grizzly Bear asked Grandfather, 'Why are you so nice to me?'

"Grandfather told her, 'We both have the right to feel safe and secure. I know that if I make this a safe place for you, then I won't have to worry about you hurting me, so I'll feel safe too.'

"Grizzly Bear said, 'Thank you, Grandfather, and you don't have to worry, because I would never do anything to hurt you, because now you are a friend.'

"As winter set in, Grandfather and Grizzly Bear found a spot that was a perfect den for her to spend the winter and to give birth to her cubs.

"Grizzly Bear settled down in her new home, and for the first time in many months she didn't have to worry about anything. She hadn't realized until then what a wonderful feeling it is to know you are completely safe. She had learned that safety is something that others can give to you but also something that others can take away.

"Early the next spring she emerged from her den with her two new cubs. She remembered what Grandfather had taught her. She promised herself that she would give her cubs a safe place to live."

Kingfisher Finds The Answer

Kingfisher sat on a tree branch looking down into the shallow water of the bay. Other birds were diving into the water and getting fish to eat.

Kingfisher thought he saw a small fish swimming around in the seaweed. He swooped down from his branch and glided over to the spot. He hovered over it for a second, and sure enough, there was the fish below him, swimming just in front of a stick. Kingfisher dove into the water and bit into something. But it wasn't the fish, it was the stick! Kingfisher couldn't believe he'd missed the fish.

He flew up into the air again and looked down. There was the little fish again. This time it was just in front of a rock. Kingfisher splashed down into the water, but instead of getting the fish, he ended up hitting the rock behind it.

Kingfisher flew back to the tree to dry out his feathers and try to figure out what he was doing wrong. As he sat there, he thought he heard someone chuckle. He looked around, and there was Raven sitting up above him.

Raven smiled at him and said, "I guess fishing is a lot tougher than it looks."

Kingfisher asked, "How come the fish is never where I think it is?"

Raven replied, "I don't know. You'll have to find that out on your own."

Kingfisher asked Raven, "How do I do that?"

Raven said, "Before you can figure out the answer, you first have to figure out what the problem is."

Kingfisher answered, "I know what the problem is. I can't catch the fish."

Raven replied, "No, the real problem you need to solve is why you can't catch the fish. Ask yourself, why does the fish look like it is in one place when it is really in another?"

Kingfisher thought about that. He remembered that both times he tried to get the fish, he had hit something behind it. Both times the fish had really been closer than it seemed.

Kingfisher flew down to the edge of a shallow pool. He looked at a small shell on the bottom and slowly reached into the water to pick it up. Sure enough, the shell was really closer to him than it looked. He didn't know why, but somehow the water was playing a trick on him.

He practised reaching for the shell in front of where it appeared, and soon he could pick it up every time.

Raven called to him, "Looks like you may have solved the problem. Now you need to take what you have learned and try it out on a fish."

Kingfisher flew up into the air. He spotted a fish, but this time he dove in a bit closer, and sure enough he came up with it in his beak. He flew back to the tree and said to Raven, "Thanks for your help."

Raven replied, "It wasn't me. You solved it on your own."

Kingfisher smiled, "You were right. The hardest part was figuring out what the problem was. Then it was easy to figure out what to do."

Ant Leads The Way

Grandfather and Grandson walked along the forest trail. They came to a small meadow and sat down by a log to enjoy their picnic lunch.

Grandfather asked, "How is that fort you started with your friends?"

Grandson replied, "Not very good. They aren't helping very much."

"Why is that?" Grandfather asked.

"I don't know," Grandson said. "It was my idea to build the fort, so I told them what I wanted them to do. When I went back the next day, they had not done it the way I told them. I got angry and told them to take it apart and do it again my way, but they said 'no' and went home."

Grandfather sat quietly for a moment and then pointed to Ant, who was crawling across their picnic blanket. He said, "Look at Ant. He is trying to carry one of our cookies back to his nest."

Grandson watched as Ant tried to lift the whole cookie and drag it along the ground. He said, "He'll never do it. It's too heavy for him to lift."

Grandfather said, "I think he's figured that out. He's asked his friends to come and help. See, Ant bit off a small piece, and now all the others are each biting off a small crumb too."

Grandson said, "But they are just running all over the place. They need someone to tell them what to do."

"Look at Ant," said Grandfather. "He's not telling them what to do, he is showing them what to do. Perhaps there is a lesson here for you, Grandson. Instead of telling your friends what to do, you need to be like Ant and show them by doing it yourself.

"Tomorrow, when your friends come to help, you should try to lead by example. Don't boss them around or yell at them. That's not what being a leader is. I think you will find that others will want to help too, and before you know it your fort will be finished."

Grandson smiled and said, "Thanks, Grandfather. I know you are right, because while we were talking, the last crumb of that cookie disappeared into Ant's nest!"

Little Mink's Big Favour

Grandmother sat watching her grandchildren play with the neighbourhood children in the yard. It was wonderful to close her eyes and just listen to the sounds of their laughter.

Out of the laughter there came one child's voice. She wasn't laughing, she was crying. Grandmother looked around and saw the little girl sitting by herself.

Grandmother called to her Granddaughter to come over and asked her, "Why is that little girl over there crying?"

"Oh," said Granddaughter, "she's sad because I made fun of her weight. She is so fat!"

Grandmother asked, "Do you think that because someone is heavier than you, they don't have the same feelings as you do?

"When I was young I remember thinking the same way you do. Then, one day I was playing with my ball. I threw it and it landed on the other side of that fence. I wasn't fat, but I still couldn't get under the fence to get it, so I thought I'd lost it. I was heartbroken. Mink came along and asked me why I was crying.

"I said, 'Because I am too big to get under the fence to get my ball.'

"Mink said to me, 'You're awfully fat, aren't you? Lucky for you I'm thin, so I can get under the fence and get your ball for you.'

"I said to Mink, 'I'm not fat!'

"Mink replied, 'I'm sorry. I didn't mean to hurt your feelings. It's just that you sure look big to me!'

"Mink easily squeezed under the fence and got my ball back for me.

"Mink said to me, 'Some of us are bigger and some of us are smaller, but we all deserve to be treated nicely.'"

Granddaughter looked over at the sad little girl.

She ran over to her and said, "I'm sorry for making fun of you. You've always been a good friend to me. I understand that we are both just the right size for who we are."

Spider's Trick

Grandmother sat on the shoreline. She had a pad of paper and a pencil on her lap. She was drawing a picture of Heron, who was standing in the shallow water hunting for food.

Grandson sat beside her, watching as the drawing flowed from the end of her pencil, like magic. He watched her eyes as they darted back and forth from the scene to the paper.

The image of Heron appeared on the paper like a bird emerging from the fog. At first Grandson could not tell what it was, but when the drawing was finished, it was so real he almost expected to see Heron move.

Grandmother tore it off the pad, folded it up, and put it in her pocket.

Grandson asked, "Why did you fold up your drawing? Aren't you going to hang it up on your wall when you get back home?"

Grandmother chuckled and said, "No, it's not for hanging up. I was just practising."

Grandson said, "I wish I could draw like you. When I finish a picture, people still can't tell what animal I was trying to do."

Grandmother said, "That's what all my drawings used to look like too. Then one day I was trying to draw a picture of Spider's web. I kept getting the lines all crooked. I said to Spider, 'How do you make the lines in your web so even?'

"Spider said, 'It took a long time, but I kept trying and finally I had an idea. If I held out one leg, I could use it to measure how far I was from my last line. Then it was easy to keep my lines the same distance apart.'

"So I tried the same thing on my picture, using my little finger to measure the distance between my lines. It worked like a charm."

Grandmother said to Grandson, "I realized that if I wanted to learn how to draw really well I'd have to keep practising, just like I was doing today. Every time I do a drawing, I learn another trick that helps make my next drawing even better."

Grandmother passed the pad and pencil to Grandson and said, "If you want to learn how to draw well, then the trick is to practise every chance you get."

Raven's Best Friend

Raven and Eagle were best friends. They had known each other since before either of them could fly. Whenever you saw one of them flying up in the clouds, you always knew the other would be soaring somewhere nearby.

One day Raven went to find Eagle so they could go flying, but Eagle wasn't in his nest. Raven flew over the forest, looking for his friend. Finally he spotted Eagle fishing with Bear along the edge of the river. Eagle and Bear were laughing and trying to splash each other, just like best friends do. Raven's feelings were hurt. How could Eagle be best friends with Bear when he was already best friends with him?

Raven asked for Grandfather's advice. "I'm very mad at Bear. He is trying to take my best friend away. Eagle is my best friend, so he shouldn't be playing with Bear," said Raven.

Grandfather asked, "What were they doing together?"

Raven replied, "Fishing in the river."

Grandfather asked Raven, "Do you like fishing?"

Raven said, "No. I hate fishing. I get all wet and cold, and the fish are all slimy. I don't know why Eagle likes to fish with Bear so much."

Grandfather pointed out, "Ah, but he does. You shouldn't try to keep Eagle and Bear from doing something they like together just because you don't like to do it."

Raven thought about that, then said, "You are right, Grandfather. Eagle and I like to fly up in the clouds, and Bear can't do that. Bear never gets mad at Eagle for flying with me, so I guess I don't have the right to be mad at Bear for fishing with Eagle."

Grandfather smiled and said, "That's a good way to look at it. Being best friends doesn't mean that you own the friend, only that you enjoy doing certain things together."

Little Bobcat's Big Adventure

Father Bobcat told Mother Bobcat that it was time for him to take Little Bobcat out into the forest to teach him how to hunt and take care of himself. They would be gone a few days, but she should not worry. She watched Little Bobcat trot off into the deep, dark forest with Father Bobcat.

Mother Bobcat didn't like the fact that Little Bobcat was growing up so fast. She preferred the little kitten he had been last spring. He would always stay nearby and wouldn't do anything unless she said it was safe.

Mother Bobcat didn't like having Little Bobcat out of her sight. She worried, "What if he gets lost?"

She didn't like not knowing what he was doing. She worried, "What if he gets hurt?"

Because of her worrying, she hardly ate or got any sleep while they were away. When they returned, she said to Little Bobcat, "You can never go into the woods again. I was so worried about you."

Father Bobcat said, "He had a wonderful adventure out on his own. He is back safely, so all your fretting was for nothing. You should be proud of him. He learned a lot while he was away."

Mother Bobcat said, "I don't care if he learned a lot. He is never allowed to be out of my sight again."

Father Bobcat said to her, "I remember your mother didn't like you growing up, either. Your Grandfather told her, 'Growing up is something all children will do whether their parents want them to or not. You cannot stop them any more than you can stop the next season from coming.'

"Now it is your turn to let Little Bobcat grow up. If you try to protect him too much, then when the time comes for him to leave, he won't know how to survive on his own. Then you truly would have something to worry about!"

Mother Bobcat nodded in agreement and said, "I promise to start letting Little Bobcat have more freedom before it comes time for him to go out on his own."

Mother Quail's Chicks

Mother Quail and her chicks had been on their own since Father Quail had left. It was hard for the chicks to understand why he now lived on the other side of the big meadow. They only saw him for a few hours when he came to visit. The Quail chicks wanted them all to be one family again.

Mother Quail told them that Father Quail would not be coming back to live with them. It made the chicks feel sad because they didn't understand why.

The chicks did know that since he had been gone, there had been more harmony in their home. They didn't find Mother Quail crying by herself, and Father Quail wasn't storming around angry all the time.

Mother Quail and Father Quail both seemed more content, and the chicks felt safer and more secure because their home was now a happier place.

Still, the little ones worried about what would happen to them now that Father Quail wasn't around very much. Mother Quail didn't have as much time to spend with them. At night she was very tired after a long day of collecting food and protecting the chicks.

The chicks started helping her whenever they could. They picked up seeds and other food they found. The bigger ones watched out for the smaller ones, to keep them safe.

One day they were out on a walk, and Mother Quail said to them, "These have been challenging days. Thank you for all your help. It makes things much easier for me when you come along to find food with me. It also makes me happy when you all watch out for each other. I love you all very much."

One of the chicks asked, "Why doesn't Father Quail love us anymore?"

Mother Quail replied, "Father Quail still loves all of you. He moved away because he wants you all to have a happy home to grow up in.

"I know it is hard to understand when you are still so young, but as you grow up I believe you will see that it was the right thing to do."

Snow fell from the grey sky and painted the forest like the stroke of an artist's brush. It transformed the world into sparkling ice and created a magical playground. Grandson wanted to go out and play.

Grandfather said, "First you need to bring in firewood from the shed."

Grandson groaned, but said, "OK. I'll bring it in before I go to play."

Outside, Grandson could hear his friends playing on the big hill. So he snuck to the back of the woodshed, grabbed his sled, and ran to the hill.

When he got home, Grandfather asked, "How come you didn't bring in the firewood like you promised?"

Grandson lied, "I did bring it in. Grandmother must have burned it all up."

Grandfather replied, "Did you see her burning wood in the stove?"

Grandson lied again, "Yes. She was cooking pies."

Grandfather sat him down and said, "When I was young, Weasel used to live out near our woodshed. One day I chopped a big pile of firewood, but when I went out the next day most of it was gone.

"I asked Weasel where it was. He lied and told me Raven had stolen it. I told him that was a lie, because Raven had been with me. Then Weasel lied again. He said it was really Eagle who had stolen my firewood. But I knew that Eagle had gone away fishing far up the river.

"Weasel knew he was caught in a trap made out of his own lies. There was no way out. He finally had to admit he had stolen my firewood."

Grandfather looked at Grandson and said, "Grandmother was in the village all morning, and I don't see any pies in the kitchen."

Grandson thought about making up another story, but he remembered how Weasel had made things worse by telling a second lie to cover up the first.

Grandson said, "I never brought in the firewood, Grandfather. I went and played in the snow all day instead. I'm sorry."

Grandfather said to him, "It took courage to tell the truth. I'm glad you learned that lying creates a trap you always get caught in."

Butterfly's Journey

A young girl found a tiny caterpillar inching its way along a twig on the alder tree that grew in the meadow. She watched it as it slowly crawled onto a leaf and started eating it.

At dinner she told Mother and Father about seeing Caterpillar on the alder tree. After they had finished eating, Father told her a story.

"You are like a little caterpillar," he said. "You started out very tiny and helpless. Each day you grow in size, wisdom, and experience.

"When you eat something, like you did at dinner, it helps you to grow taller. When you see something, like you saw Caterpillar today, it makes you wiser. When you do something, like you will tomorrow, it makes you more experienced."

The young girl asked, "What am I going to do tomorrow?"

He replied, "Tomorrow I want you to start watching Caterpillar. Go out to the meadow each day and draw pictures of her and write down how she changes."

For the next few weeks Granddaughter went out and found Caterpillar on the tree and did drawings of her. Each day Caterpillar grew bigger and was changing in colour and shape.

One day she went out and couldn't find Caterpillar. Mother came to help her look. Mother pointed at a small cocoon hanging from a twig.

"That's Caterpillar," she said. "She's been growing up, and now it's time for her to move on to the next phase of her life."

The young girl continued to watch the cocoon. One day it split apart, and a beautiful butterfly struggled its way out.

Butterfly stretched her wings and let them dry in the warm sunshine. Then she fluttered off across the meadow and into the distance.

The girl was sad to see her go, but she was glad she had seen her change from a little caterpillar into an adult butterfly.

Father said to her, "Right now you are still like a little caterpillar, growing, learning, and gaining experience. But one day these changes will all come together, and you will find that you are ready to fly off too."

Octopus Learns to Share

Grandmother had made a birthday cake for Granddaughter to take to school to share with the other children.

All the children were excited and wanted a piece of the cake, but as Granddaughter started to cut it into pieces, the children that were closest reached out and snatched them off the plate before she could give them to everyone. Some of the children got two pieces and others got none.

She cried, "Next time I won't bring my birthday cake to share with you."

Teacher sat all the children down and said, "Watching all of you reach out to try and get more than your share of cake reminds me of Octopus, whose tentacles learned the hard way about the importance of sharing.

"Octopus was wandering along the bottom of the sea looking for something to eat. One of her favourite foods was crab, which live near the reef. As she came over a pile of stones she saw one, but it saw her too and dashed into one of the cracks between the rocks.

"Octopus looked in and could see the crab hiding, so her eight tentacles all tried to reach in and get it. Each tentacle went into a different hole in the pile of stones and grabbed hold of the crab.

"That's when the problem started. When one tentacle tried to pull out the crab, the others all tried to do the same. No matter how hard each one pulled, none of them could get the crab out.

"Octopus realized her problem and told her tentacles to all let go of the crab. But when they did, the crab immediately scurried deeper into the pile of stones, beyond their reach.

"Octopus's tentacles had learned that if you don't share, then someday you will be the one who ends up with nothing."

The children who had more than one piece of cake apologized to Granddaughter and gave their extra pieces to the children who didn't have any. Everyone was happy.

Skunk's Smell

It was one of those calm summer days that is perfect for going out in a boat and fishing on the lake. Younger Brother was excited about going out and trying to catch a big fish.

He and Older Brother packed up lunches. Older Brother picked up his fishing rod from the corner of the porch.

"Where is my fishing rod?" Younger Brother asked him. "I left it on the porch with yours, like I always do, and now it's gone. You must have borrowed it and never brought it back!" he shouted.

"I didn't take it," shouted Older Brother. "Maybe last time you left it somewhere else."

Younger Brother was sure Older Brother must have taken it, so in anger he grabbed Older Brother's fishing rod. As he did he tripped and fell and broke it in half.

Now the two of them were shouting back and forth at each other. All the noise caused Grandfather to come out to see what was going on.

He asked, "Why are you yelling at each other?"

Older Brother said, "I'm angry because he broke my fishing rod."

Younger Brother said, "It was an accident. I'm yelling because he took my fishing rod and lost it."

Grandfather sighed and said to Younger Brother, "Remember you went out fishing with me yesterday, and you decided to leave your rod in the boat? That's where your fishing rod is."

Younger Brother felt ashamed. He had accused Older Brother of something he didn't do and, to make things worse, he had broken his fishing rod.

Grandfather sat the two boys down and said to Younger Brother, "You need to be careful if you are going to accuse someone, because if you are wrong it can leave more than just hurt feelings.

"Once I thought Skunk had stolen some vegetables from my garden. The next time I saw him I accused him of taking them.

"Skunk replied, 'I haven't been anywhere near your garden.'

"I shouted at him, 'You are lying. You have to bring them back.'

"Skunk got angry and said, 'I can't bring them back because I never took them in the first place.'

"I picked up a stone and threw it at Skunk. I missed him, but he got scared and sprayed me with his horrible-smelling scent, then ran away.

"I went down to my garden to use the hose to try and wash away the smell, and when I got there, who do you think I found taking my vegetables?"

Younger Brother guessed, "I bet it was Skunk!"

Grandfather replied, "No, it wasn't Skunk. It was Grandmother. She had been picking some of the vegetables to share with one of the neighbours.

"She asked me, 'Why do you smell like Skunk sprayed you?'

"I replied, 'Because Skunk *did* spray me.'

"She asked, 'Now why would he do that? I thought you two were friends.'

"I admitted what I had done, and she said, 'Well, it serves you right. Now, what are you going to do to fix the mess you have made?'

"I went and found Skunk and apologized to him. I gave him some of my vegetables to try to make things better.

"Skunk said he forgave me, but that didn't make the terrible smell go away.

"I smelled for days, and all I had was myself to blame. Skunk's smell helped me remember the hard lesson I had learned. The way you choose to react to a situation can make it much worse instead of better.

"Even today, when I think of accusing anyone, I remember that smell. It reminds me to be very sure of my facts."

Younger Brother said to Older Brother, "I'm sorry. And I'm sorry that I broke your rod. Will you forgive me if I buy you a new one?"

Older Brother said, "I forgive you, but you'll have to live with the fact that the stink you raised made things worse instead of better. That's a smell you'll have to live with for quite a while."

Steelhead's Way

The cold water from snow melting high up in the mountains flowed down the creek behind Grandfather's home, where he and Grandson sat talking.

Grandson said, "I feel like I don't belong here. I don't believe in the same things as most of the other children, so I don't feel like I can be friends with them. And they don't seem to want to be friends with me either.

"As soon as I am old enough I'm going to move far away from here to a place where I feel welcome."

Grandfather said to him, "Running away from a problem won't work. You need to find a way to help everyone, including yourself, to understand that it is important to respect and accept other ways of looking at things."

Grandfather pointed and said, "Look, down there in the water."

In among the stones at the bottom of the creek, small orange eggs were starting to hatch into tiny fish.

Grandfather said, "Those are rainbow trout. Even though they all look similar now, some of them are different because they will become steelhead trout."

Grandson asked, "How does that happen, Grandfather?"

Grandfather said, "Many years ago when Rainbow Trout first arrived, she came up this creek to lay her eggs.

"The baby trout grew quickly as the creek's water brought the insects and other food they needed. By summer, all the little trout swam out of the creek and into the big lake, where there was more food and it was safer.

"But two of the trout were not happy in the lake and wanted to try living in the ocean, like salmon do.

"The other trout said, 'We believe all trout are supposed to live in lakes.'

"The two trout replied, 'We don't believe that. We think trout should be able to live in the ocean too.'

"All the other trout couldn't understand why these two chose to believe that. They teased and made fun of them. This made the two trout feel unwelcome, so they left and swam downriver to try living in the ocean.

"In the ocean they tried to join a school of salmon, but because they were different, the salmon didn't make them feel welcome either. Because they didn't feel welcome in the lake or the ocean, the only place left was the river.

"So they swam back there and became strong steelhead trout, because they had to be tough to swim in the swift river currents. But they were lonely.

"One year when the big lake flooded, some of the rainbow trout got swept into the river. They were carried downriver until the two steelhead trout saw them. The steelhead trout helped them find their way back upstream to their home in the lake.

"One of the rainbow trout said to them, 'Thank goodness you two were in the river when we needed your help. We are sorry that we didn't make you feel welcome in the lake. You have helped us understand the importance of accepting those who have different ideas.'

"One of the steelhead trout replied, 'We also learned that if you believe in different things, you have to help others to understand, instead of just running away from them.'"

Grandson looked up at Grandfather and said, "That's a good lesson. Tomorrow I'm going to make an effort to make friends with the others. I need to learn how to respect their point of view and help them understand mine. I'm not going to be like the two steelhead trout and run away from those who don't think the way I do."

Duck's Discovery

It was late spring, and the school year had come to a close. All the children looked forward to summer vacation. But summertime also meant they would all move on to a new class when they went back in the fall.

Granddaughter had become good friends with many of the children in this year's class. She liked her teacher, who was very helpful, and she liked this classroom with its rows of good books along the back wall.

All the way home from school she thought about the changes that were coming. The more she thought about them the more upset she felt. By suppertime she didn't even feel like eating.

After supper she looked for Grandfather and found him sitting on the porch swing. She sat down to talk with him about how bad she was feeling.

"Did you ever wish things would just stay the way they are forever?" she asked Grandfather.

"Why do you ask that?" replied Grandfather.

"When we go back to school after the holidays, we all have to move on to a new class. I'm worried that if my friends are not in my class next year I'll lose them.

"I'm also afraid my new teacher won't be as kind as the one I had this year. And, what if my new classroom doesn't have any interesting books to read?"

Grandfather said to her, "Sometimes, even when we think we are not ready, it is time to move on.

"I remember when I was young, watching Little Mallard Duck and his 10 brothers and sisters grow up in the pond.

"All that summer they played together with the other pond birds. They all kept each other company and became best of friends. Mother Mallard Duck was their teacher, and she taught them how to fly and find food. And, at night they would gather together in their warm, safe nest to sleep.

"But, as the weather started to change, Mother Mallard Duck knew it would soon be time to fly south to find a new home for the winter.

"Little Mallard Duck said, 'I'm not going! I like this pond, where I know all the other birds I have made friends with. I know where to find food on the bottom of the pond. And I don't want to leave the nest I was born in.'

"For days Mother Mallard Duck tried to convince him to accept the change and come with the rest of them. But Little Mallard Duck refused to go.

"As the icy winds of winter started to blow, Mother Mallard Duck could not wait any longer, so she took the other 10 ducklings and left Little Mallard behind.

"It turned out to be a very hard winter for Little Mallard Duck. All the other birds migrated south, so he was left all alone on the pond. Then the water froze over, and he couldn't find very much food to eat. Finally snow fell and covered up his nest, so he had to spend his nights just trying to find a place to keep warm.

"I felt sorry for him, so I made him a small nest in our woodshed. I visited him every couple of days, so he wouldn't be too lonely. And I brought him some grain, so he had something to eat.

"When spring finally came, Mother Mallard Duck and the other ducklings arrived back at the pond. Little Mallard Duck raced down to greet them.

"Little Mallard Duck told them, 'I am so glad to see you again! I was so lonely and cold and hungry without you.'

"His brothers and sisters said to him, 'You should have come with us. We missed you. Our winter home was warm, we met lots of new friends, and we always had lots to eat.'

"That fall Little Mallard Duck happily went south with his family and the rest of the birds who lived at the pond. Little Mallard Duck had discovered that you have to accept that things change over time, because if you don't, the rest of the world will move on without waiting for you."

Granddaughter thought about the lesson Little Mallard Duck had learned.

She said to Grandfather, "Thanks for telling me about Little Mallard Duck. It's time for me to move on, too. If I don't accept the changes that are coming, the rest of my friends, my teachers, and my family will have to move on and leave me behind."

Heron's Rule

Grandson and Grandfather were walking along the path by the shore of the lake. It was quiet in the forest, and they enjoyed the peaceful view across the water, with its sparkling surface dancing in the light breeze.

They stopped to rest on a big rock. Just offshore, two herons stood among the reeds, not making a sound.

Grandfather noticed that the boy wasn't as cheerful as usual and said, "You are as quiet as those herons out there. Normally on our walks you're always asking me questions, but today you haven't said a word."

Grandson replied, "I've been thinking about a friend of mine. I'm worried about him."

Grandfather said, "Tell me why you feel that way."

Grandson remembered promising his friend never to tell anyone about this secret. He'd always kept his promise before, and his friend had done the same for the secrets Grandson had shared with him.

Grandson said, "I'm sorry, but I can't tell you, Grandfather. My friend told me to keep it a secret. He trusted me not to tell anyone else.

"The problem is, if I don't tell someone else, it will probably get worse. But if I do tell, my friend may never trust me again."

Grandfather thought about what Grandson had said. He decided to help him by telling him a story.

He said to Grandson, "When I am faced with that kind of decision I always use the rule Heron taught me."

"What's Heron's rule?" asked Grandson.

Grandfather replied, "Heron once had a friend who told him lots of secrets. Most of the secrets were about things like good places to fish or where he liked to go to find a safe place to rest. He would also tell him personal secrets, like the one about a pretty heron that he really liked a lot.

"Heron never told a soul about any of the secrets his friend had trusted to tell him. And his friend always kept the secrets Heron shared with him.

"But one day Heron's friend told him another kind of secret and, for the first time, Heron had to decide if he would tell someone else about it.

"His friend had told him that he was being hurt by a grown-up. The grown-up had told him never to tell anyone, but Heron's friend had decided to tell him only because he trusted Heron to keep it a secret."

Grandson asked, "So, how did he decide if this was the type of secret he should tell someone else about?"

Grandfather replied, "Heron had a rule about keeping secrets. When he had to make a decision about telling someone's secret, he would find a very quiet place, just like this one, where he could hear the voice inside him. That voice would tell him the right thing to do.

"Heron asked himself, 'Is it better to keep my friend's secret or for my friend to keep on getting hurt?'

"This time the voice told him that the right thing to do was to have the courage to break his promise, rather than see his friend continue getting hurt.

"Heron flew home to his parents' nest and told them the secret. They made sure that the grown-up never hurt his friend again.

"Although his friend's feelings were hurt because Heron had broken his promise, he was very happy he did not have to worry about being hurt any more. He forgave Heron, and they are still friends today."

Grandson thought about the story. He asked himself, "What is the right thing for me to do?" The voice inside him said, "You need to tell Grandfather the secret before your friend is hurt again. You may lose a friend, but if your friend keeps getting hurt, you could lose him anyway."

Grandson said to Grandfather, "Thank you for telling me about Heron's rule. I'm going to tell you my friend's secret, because I know that, in this case, it is the right thing to do."

Owl's Solution

Grandson and his friends sat on a log on the beach. Owl sat in the tree above them, listening to them talk about how dirty the beach was. They could not agree on who should clean it up.

One child said, "It's the people who go out fishing and dump their garbage over the side of their boat. They should have to clean this up."

Another said, "No. It's all the older kids who come to the beach and leave their garbage behind when they leave. They should clean it up."

One of them said, "*Somebody* needs to clean it up."

Owl flew down and landed beside them. He asked, "Who is this mysterious person, called 'somebody,' who is going to clean up the beach?"

None of the children knew exactly who "somebody" was, but one replied, "I don't know who it is, but I do know it's not me, because it's not my garbage."

Another child said, "I'm not going to do it either. Even if I did drop some of the garbage I'm not going to clean up everyone else's."

All the rest said that it wasn't going to be any of them either.

Owl said to them, "Then the problem will only get worse. If you're not willing to help find a solution, then doesn't that make each of you part of the problem?

"The only way a problem like this ever goes away is if each one of you takes on at least some responsibility for solving it."

Grandson said to the rest of the group, "I'm going to pick up a couple of handfuls of garbage every time I come to the beach. By the end of the summer at least some of the garbage will be gone."

Another child nodded and said, "Hey, that's a good idea. I'll help you. With two of us picking it up it will get cleaned up twice as fast."

The rest wanted to help too. Every time they came down to the beach they all picked up some of the paper and bottles. Within a few weeks they had the beach back to the way it used to be.

They all agreed that Owl had been right. Problems only go away when each of us becomes part of the solution.

Mountain Sheep's Tunnel

Eagle flew overhead, watching a young boy below. The boy was trying hard to drag a large log from the forest to the woodshed.

Eagle asked him, "Why don't you cut the log into small pieces?"

The boy replied, "It's faster to carry one big piece than to make lots of trips back and forth. I want to finish in time to go swimming with my friends."

Eagle said, "Let me tell you the story of Mountain Sheep.

"Mountain Sheep lived on the rocky slopes at the bottom of a big mountain. He had a huge set of curled horns that he loved to butt with.

"One day his father asked him to go to the next valley to see if the spring grass was ready to eat. Mountain Sheep decided that instead of going around or over the mountain, he would try to go through it.

"He started butting into the rock, and slowly pieces started to crumble to the ground. He quickly realized that this was going to be much harder than he thought, but he was too stubborn to admit he was wrong. He continued breaking rock, and eventually he broke through the last bit of it and stepped into the sunshine. To his surprise his father was standing there waiting for him.

"His father said, 'In the time it took you to break a tunnel through the mountain I was able to walk around it. You are tired and your horns are all chipped and broken. I had an enjoyable walk, and had time to eat lots of nice grass while I waited for you.'

"Mountain Sheep replied, 'You are right. I was too stubborn to see that the shortest way is not always the fastest way to get to where you are going.'"

The boy looked at the big log and thought about what Mountain Sheep had discovered. He took his saw and began cutting the log into small pieces.

Eagle smiled at him and asked, "I thought you were going to save time by dragging the whole log to the woodshed?"

The boy smiled back and said, "I've learned from your story that in the time it would take me to drag the whole log, I could cut it up, carry it, stack it, and still have time to go swimming with my friends."

Dogwood's Day

A droplet of water high up in the spring sky fell from the clouds toward earth. As it fell the air got colder and colder until the raindrop froze into a delicate, floating crystal of snow. Finally it came to rest on Grandmother's hand, where it quickly melted away.

Grandmother was reminded of the story of Dogwood Tree.

She looked down at Granddaughter and said, "Remember yesterday when you were complaining about how dark and cold it is in wintertime?"

Granddaughter replied, "Yes. I like these warm days better."

Grandmother said to her, "When I was growing up, everyone in our village always complained about the weather. In wintertime they would say there was too much snow, in springtime it rained too much. In summer it was too hot and in autumn it was frosty.

"One bright summer morning some people were about to cut down a dogwood tree for firewood and, as usual, were complaining that it was too hot.

"Raven listened to them and decided to give them a lesson to remind them to stop complaining and enjoy the nice weather.

"He flew down to the pond and soaked his feathers with water, then flew high up into the cold air and shook the water from his wings. As the droplets fell they froze into snowflakes and drifted down to earth to settle on the leaves of the dogwood tree that the people were about to cut down.

"All of the people felt the chill of the snow and backed away from Dogwood Tree. As they did, they again felt the warmth of the summer's sun. That was when they first realized they had not been enjoying the fine summer day.

"The snow that Raven made never melted off the leaves of Dogwood Tree. So the people decided they would leave the tree standing as a reminder."

Grandmother pointed to Dogwood Tree out in the meadow, with its frosting of snow-white leaves surrounding its tiny yellow flowers and said, "Dogwood Tree is still here to remind us to enjoy every nice day we are given."

About the Author

Born in Vancouver, British Columbia, in 1953, Robert James (Jim) Challenger lives in Victoria, on the southern end of Vancouver Island.

Jim has spent his life absorbing all the stories the Northwest Coast has to offer. A keen observer of the natural behaviour of wildlife, he has developed his own style of artwork that captures the essence of the many creatures that live around him.

Jim is an accomplished artist and stone carver, and has sold his beach-stone and glass carvings to collectors around the world. His highly sought-after form-line designs capture the shape and movement of his subjects while maintaining the simplicity of flowing lines and shapes.

Jim's stories and designs bring a unique perspective to how we can learn from nature's examples in the world that surrounds us. For more information about the author, you can visit his website: http://www.rjchallenger.com